HENRY BEAR'S PARK

HENRY BEAR'S PARK

BY

DAVID McPHAIL

Puffin Books

For Stanley Dixon, the original Stanley

Penguin Books Ltd, Harmondsworth, Middlesex, England
Penguin Books, 625 Madison Avenue, New York, New York 10022, U.S.A.
Penguin Books Australia Ltd, Ringwood, Victoria, Australia
Penguin Books Canada Limited, 2801 John Street, Markham, Ontario, Canada L3R 1B4
Penguin Books (N.Z.) Ltd, 182–190 Wairau Road, Auckland 10, New Zealand

First published by Little, Brown and Company, Inc., 1976
Reprinted by arrangement with Little, Brown and Company
in association with the Atlantic Monthly Press
Published in Puffin Books 1978

Library of Congress Cataloging in Publication Data
McPhail, David M.   Henry Bear's park.
Summary: Henry Bear takes good care of the park that
his father bought before taking off on a balloon trip.
[1. Bears—Fiction] I. Title.
PZ7.M2427He 1978   [E]   78-59683
ISBN 0 14 050. 291 2

Printed in the United States of America by
Rae Publishing Co., Inc., Cedar Grove, New Jersey
Set in Bembo

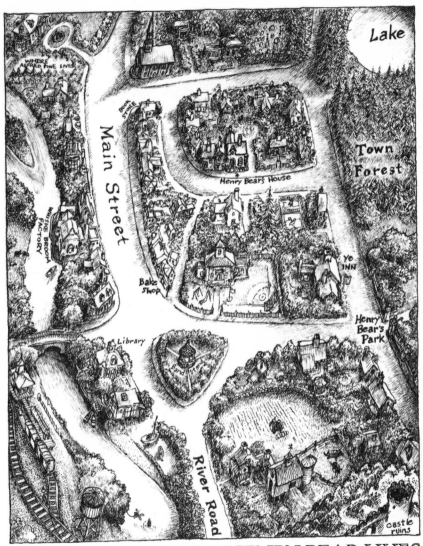

THE TOWN WHERE HENRY BEAR LIVES

HENRY BEAR lived with his mother and father in a comfortable little house near the center of town. Behind the house was a small garden where Henry spent many hours helping his father, whom he admired very much.

7

Henry Bear's father was a balloon ascensionist. One day, while making a tethered test flight, Poppa Bear noticed a FOR SALE sign over the entrance to the park that lay at the edge of town.

"I must have that park!" said Poppa Bear. So he sold his Stutz Bearcat and with the proceeds of the sale he bought the park.

"I always wanted to own a park," said Poppa Bear to Henry Bear. "Take good care of it while I'm gone!"

Then he climbed into his gondola, untied the tether rope and ascended.

Early the next morning Henry Bear began taking good care of his father's park. Henry Bear's mother brought him little jelly cakes for lunch and told him nice things about his father.

"He was always so at home in the air!" said Momma Bear.

13

Henry Bear enjoyed taking care of the park, even though it was hard work and it meant giving up his Tuesday afternoon cello lesson. He mowed the lawns, weeded the gardens, and trimmed the shrubs. He took away all the *Keep Off the Grass* signs and painted out the *No* on the *No Wading* sign that was bolted to the fountain. Then he pulled down the *No Visitors* sign at the entrance to the park.

15

After that, Henry Bear's park had many visitors. Happy visitors. Neat visitors. In fact, the only litter that Henry ever found was a letter to the Bureau of Missing Persons from Momma Bear. The letter contained a rather vague description of Henry Bear's father.

Under Henry's care the once dreary park became a beautiful place. Colorful gardens were surrounded by lush lawns and well-pruned trees. As time went by, however, Henry found it more and more difficult to keep up with the mowing and weeding, so he placed an advertisement in the Help Wanted section of the *Daily Gazette*.

"Wanted," read the ad, "Someone to help. Apply in person at Henry Bear's Park. Ask for Henry."

The only applicant was a raccoon named Stanley. Henry Bear liked him and hired him.

17

In order to be more on top of things at the park, Henry and Stanley built a tree house and moved in.

Momma Bear was very sad.

"First your father blew away," she moaned, "and now you! Whatever am I to do?"

"Well," consoled Henry, "you can still bring us jelly cakes. That is, if you want to . . ."

"Goodness knows what you'll eat if I don't," said Momma Bear.

Henry Bear was happy in his new home. It was a simple place, to be sure, but exactly right for Henry. With a soft easychair, a footstool, and all his books, he was quite cozy and content.

Henry felt that Poppa Bear would be pleased to know that he had finally gotten his feet off the ground.

Henry Bear spent his days working in the flower gardens, wishing visitors a pleasant day, and pointing out the best places for picnics. On rainy days he stood under the umbrella tree playing his cello for anyone who would listen.

Evening was Henry Bear's favorite time of day. He would stroll through the park whistling in response to a nightingale's song, stopping now and again to sniff the night air.

It was on one such evening stroll that Henry Bear met Alfred Pine, who introduced himself as a Yorkshire hog of considerable education. Besides being a very smart dresser, he claimed to be something of a world traveler.

"I'm just back from the Orient," said Alfred, "where the monsoon mud is most elegant!"

Alfred opened the photo album that he always carried with him.

"Here I am in Singapore," he said, pointing to a Coca-Cola sign. "And here I am on top of Tentweather Peak. It's the world's tallest mountain, you know!"

Henry Bear didn't know, but he was glad that Alfred thought he did. Henry just said "Ummm-mmmmmmm . . ."

Alfred Pine went on with his stories, turning the pages of his album and occasionally allowing Henry a glimpse at whatever he was describing. It seemed to Henry there was no place in the world that Alfred Pine hadn't been.

"Perhaps," said Henry, when Alfred finally closed the album and paused long enough for Henry to speak, "perhaps you know where my father is!"

"Your father," mused Alfred. "Ah, yes, of course, your father."

"Yes," agreed Henry, "My father! Do you know where he is, or where he went?"

"Well," said Alfred, as he threw back his shoulders and tucked in his chin, "I suppose your father *is* where he went. And as to where he went, why, that must be where he is!"

Henry was so puzzled by what Alfred said and so overwhelmed by the important way he said it that he could not speak.

Alfred excused himself. "Humppff!" he declared as he disappeared into the shadows outside the park.

Henry Bear lay awake all that night thinking of what Alfred Pine had said. *He is where he went, and he went where he is.* The sun was beginning to rise and Henry realized that he still didn't know quite where to find his father.

"I'll ask Alfred Pine to point out my father's exact location," decided Henry.

So every time he took his evening stroll, Henry carried his globe with him.

31

Several weeks passed before Alfred Pine re-
turned to the park. After a brief exchange of pleas-
antries, Henry got right to the point.

"Please," said Henry, holding up his globe,
"show me exactly where my father is."

Alfred Pine rubbed his chin nervously.

"You must understand," he said. "There are
matters about which I am sworn to secrecy."

"Well," replied Henry, "if you can't show me
where he is, perhaps, just perhaps, you could take
me to him!"

"Perhaps," grunted Pine. "But just perhaps."

33

From that moment on, Henry spent most of his time preparing for the trip. He grew neglectful in his duties at the park. The flowers wilted in spite of Stanley's heroic efforts to keep them watered, and weeds threatened to take over the lawns. The fountain became covered with green slime and stopped working. The nightingale took its song elsewhere, and the visitors found other places to visit. The park looked shabbier than it did when Henry first came there.

"What would your father say?!" scolded Momma Bear. Henry longed to tell her about his probable trip with Alfred Pine, but he didn't want to get her hopes up.

Momma Bear was so disgusted with Henry that she refused to bring him any more jelly cakes.

"Not another crumb," she declared, "until you come to your senses!"

If Henry wanted any more jelly cakes he would have to walk to the village bakeshop for them.

Henry was on his way to the bakeshop one day when he caught sight of Alfred Pine coming out of the B. B. Whiske broom factory showroom.

"Hello, Alfred Pine," called Henry, as he ran to catch up with Alfred.

When Alfred heard Henry's voice he stopped suddenly and stared straight ahead, and Henry, in his haste, ran right into him.

39

"What a handsome whisk broom you have there," said Henry.

Alfred looked desperately unhappy. Instantly Henry thought of his father.

"Is it my father?" he asked. "Has something awful happened to him?"

"Not to your father," Alfred Pine replied sadly, "to you!"

"To me?" said Henry. "Something awful has happened to me?"

"Yes," sighed Alfred mournfully. "Me."

Now Henry was more befuddled than ever.

"You see," said Alfred Pine, "I'm not really an educated Yorkshire hog. I'm a plain everyday pig from Essex, and what little traveling I've done has been from an armchair."

Then with a deep sigh he added: "I'm a butler!"

"A butler!" exclaimed Henry. "You mean someone who opens doors, and takes coats and hats from important people?"

"And whisks lint off their cloaks and capes," added Alfred.

"But you *do* know my father," insisted Henry. "Don't you?"

"That's the saddest, most horrendous part of all," answered Alfred. "I have never even seen your father!"

"Oh," said Henry, "you've talked with him on the telephone, then?"

"No! No! No!" screeched Alfred. "No telephone! No telegram! No nothing!"

"Then how do you know where he is?" asked Henry. "And where he went?"

"I don't know where he is, or where he went!" shouted Alfred. "I don't even know where he was, or where he used to be!"

"No matter," said Henry. "When we go to see him, if perhaps, just perhaps, I might come along —we'll find out all of those things!"

Alfred began to wave his whisk broom.

"If only I'd never gone to that park of yours," moaned Alfred. "If only I'd gone to the theater instead!"

"Then," declared Henry, "I might never have known about my father!"

"Your father! Your father!" Alfred screamed at the top of his voice. "For all I know your father is dangling from the church spire!"

At that very instant there arose a great commotion from across the street in front of the church.

"It's a balloon!" yelled someone from the crowd. "And a gondola!"

"It's Henry Bear, Senior!" shouted everyone in unison.

"Poppa!" cried Henry Bear, Junior. "Poppa, it's me, Henry Bear, Junior!"

"I know very well who you are!" roared Henry Bear, Senior. "Now get me down from here!"

As he ran across the street to the church, Henry Bear called over his shoulder to Alfred Pine.

"You're wonderful, Alfred Pine! Absolutely wonderful!"

Using a tall ladder and a strong rope, Henry Bear was able to rescue his father, and retrieve the balloon.

With Poppa Bear safely home, Henry once again turned his attention to the park, and in no time at all it was more beautiful than ever.

Poppa Bear spent most of his time at the park, and every day Momma Bear brought jelly cakes for lunch.